A LITTLE
SPACE
FOR ME

JENNIFER GRAY OLSON

E

ROARING BROOK PRESS

NEW YORK

Sometimes my life
feels very crowded.

CLINK
CLANK
PLINK

Sometimes it's too loud.

Or messy.

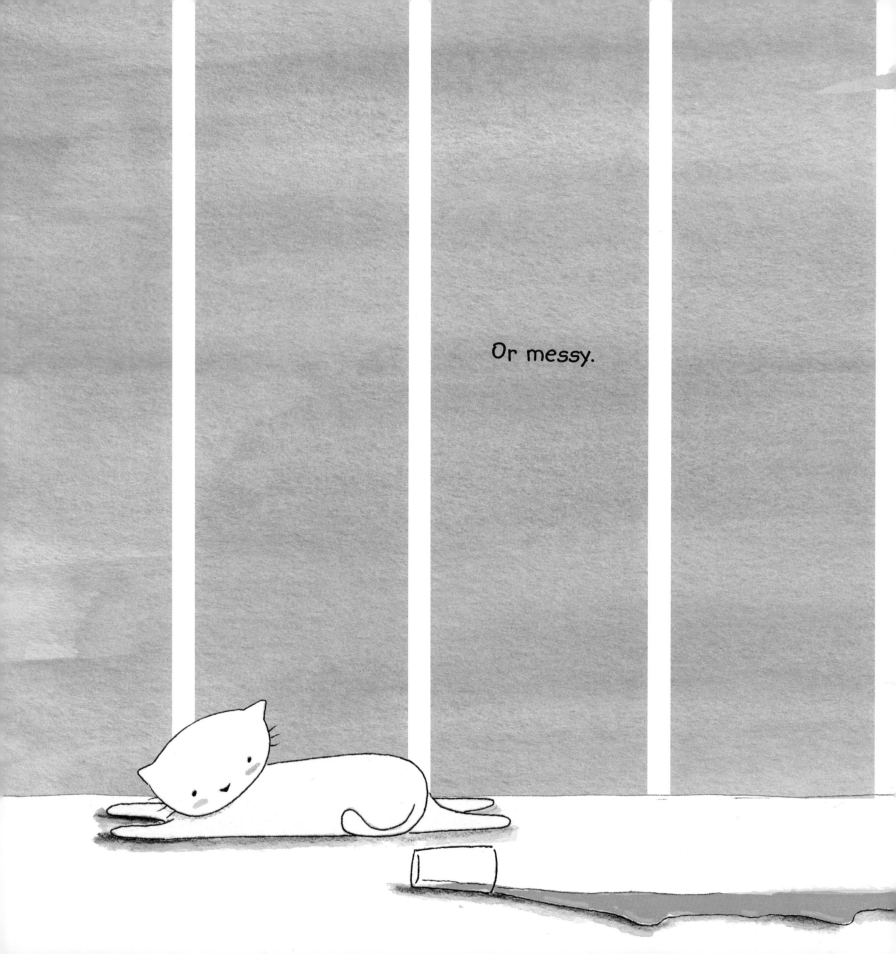

Or too hot or smelly or scratchy or bright.

Sometimes it can just be too much
for no reason at all.

One day, I decided . . .

I needed some SPACE.

So I got some.

I loved my **SPACE** so much . . .

I wanted more.

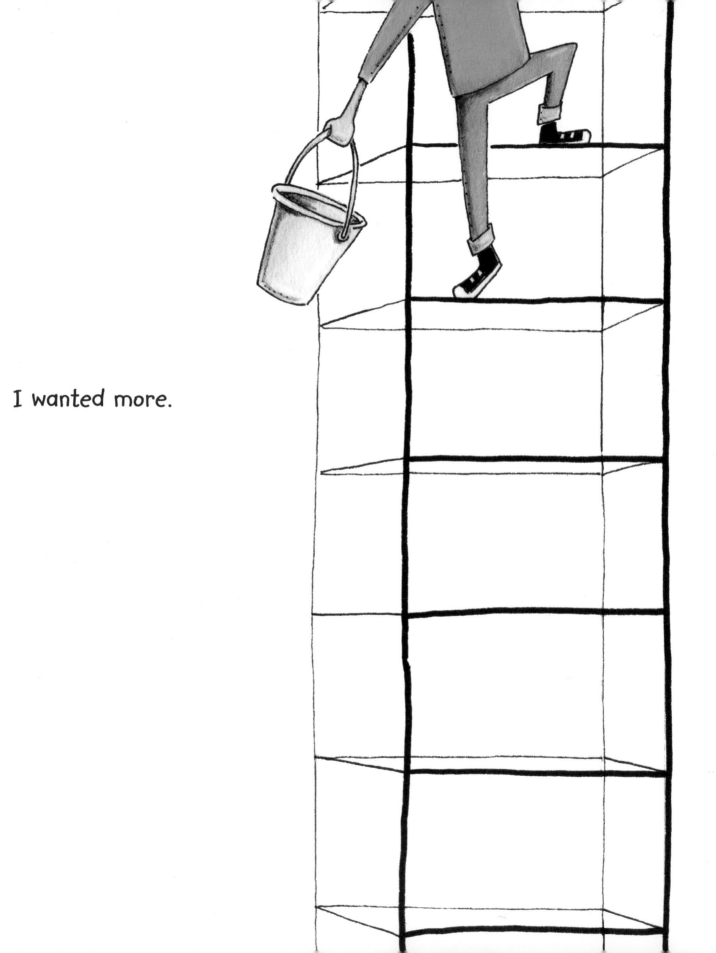

And more . . .

And even more.

Until there wasn't much **SPACE** for anything else.

At last, I had all the SPACE I needed.

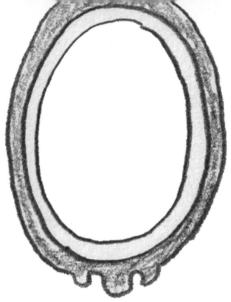

Until finally . . .

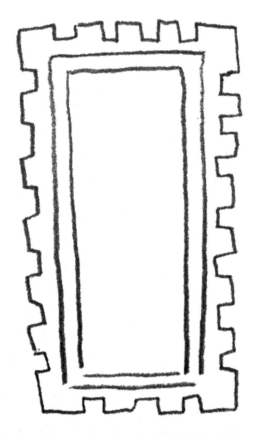

I decided to share my **SPACE**.

But I always keep a little bit with me . . .

Because everybody needs a
little **SPACE** sometimes.

To those who share my space

Library of Congress Control Number: 2019948811

Our books may be purchased in bulk for promotional, educational, or business use. Please contact your local bookseller or the Macmillan
Corporate and Premium Sales Department at (800) 221-7945 ext. 5442 or by email at MacmillanSpecialMarkets@macmillan.com.

First edition, 2020 • Book design by Aurora Parlagreco
Printed in China by Toppan Leefung Printing Ltd., Dongguan City, Guangdong Province

1 3 5 7 9 10 8 6 4 2